# Tickin' Clocks

Written by: Willie S.

© Copyright 2026 Willie S.: All Rights Reserved.

# Contents

# Dedication

This book is dedicated to the everyday people who work hard, often without recognition, and whose efforts support our society. It honors those who have faced unfairness and hardship but continue to hope and strive for a better future. This is for those who dream of a world where everyone has equal opportunities and can pursue their passions without being held back. It's a tribute to those who stand up for fairness and justice, even when it's difficult. Their strength and determination inspire this story and remind us all of the power we have to create a more just and equal world.

Part 1: The Seed of Discontent

The Money War

The storm raged outside, battering the panoramic windows of Kevin Henden's thirtieth-floor apartment, each drop a drumbeat matching the restless pulse within his chest. Lightning flashed in the distance, illuminating the jagged skyline of London—a city ablaze with affluence, its towers shimmering like beacons against the brooding sky. Yet, as the thunder rolled, Kevin saw not just the city's opulent heights but its shadowed recesses: the huddled shapes on rain-slicked sidewalks, the darkened doorways where hope flickered uncertainly. The city below was a living paradox, a contradiction that pressed ever more urgently on his conscience.

Kevin stood before the glass, hands knotted behind his back, his reflection superimposed over the golden sprawl of London. He had carved a life for himself in the upper echelons of finance, his days spent in the rarefied air of executive meetings, his nights awash with the glow of data and graphs. On paper, he was a success—a financial analyst at one of London's most prestigious firms, an architect of fortune and strategy. Yet lately, the numbers blurred, their precision mocking. He felt out of sync with the world he had helped build, as though he stood on the wrong side of a chasm he could no longer ignore.

A Life Built on Numbers

Born in the industrial outskirts of Birmingham, Kevin's ascent had been anything but guaranteed. His father had worked double shifts in a steel mill that vanished with the last recession, his mother juggling odd jobs to keep the family afloat. The scarcity of his childhood had bred a relentless drive, a hunger for stability and recognition. University had been his way out—a hard-won scholarship, all-night study sessions, a stubborn refusal to accept defeat. He learned to speak the language of capital, to navigate the labyrinthine systems of finance where fortunes were made and lost in the span of a heartbeat.

Yet success brought its own burdens. In the manicured offices of the firm, Kevin wore tailored suits and spoke the polished dialect of the privileged, but he never shook the feeling that he was a guest at someone else's table, tolerated but not truly accepted. His colleagues toasted market victories with vintage champagne, their laughter echoing down corridors lined with abstract art, while Kevin's thoughts drifted to his family's tiny flat, to the ache of hunger and the cold that crept beneath the door in winter.

Daily Observations: A City of Contrasts

Each morning, Kevin crossed the city in a black cab, eyes absorbing the theater of London in motion. He passed the glittering boutiques of Mayfair, their windows lit with jewelry that cost more than his parents' home, then drifted through neighborhoods where children in secondhand coats waited for buses beside shuttered shops. The randomness of fate gnawed at him—the invisible lottery that determined who would rise and who would be trampled beneath the grinding wheel of progress.

He began to linger on street corners, watching the ebb and flow of life. A banker in an Italian suit stepped over a sleeping figure wrapped in a tattered blanket, his gaze fixed on the glowing promise of his smartphone. In the park, a young couple debated which restaurant to try while a woman spooned soup into a child's mouth with trembling hands. Kevin was haunted by these juxtapositions, the silent testimonies of a system that rewarded a few and ignored the many.

Professional Insights: Unraveling the System

At his desk, Kevin dissected financial reports with surgical precision. He mapped the currents of capital, tracing their passage from hedge funds to offshore accounts, across borders and back again. The patterns he saw were not random. They told a story—one of power concentrated in the hands of a self-perpetuating caste. The same names surfaced again and again, their portfolios swelling as ordinary people's prospects withered.

He noticed how the rules bent for some and snapped for others. A single clause in a trade agreement, obscure to the uninitiated, meant millions in profit for a well-placed investor. A sudden regulatory shift shuttered an entire industry in the Midlands, erasing livelihoods overnight. The mechanisms were hidden behind walls of jargon, but to Kevin, the intent was all too clear: the system was designed not just to favor the wealthy, but to actively exclude those without access or influence.

Catalyst Event: The Encounter in the Rain

Everything changed the night he met her. The storm had driven most pedestrians indoors, but Kevin, restless and unable to sleep, wandered the city's side streets, letting the rain soak through his coat. On the steps of a shuttered shop, he spotted a young woman curled into herself, her thin jacket no match for the cold. She did not beg or speak. He hesitated, then ducked into a corner café for two coffees and a sandwich, more out of instinct than conscious intent.

When he offered them, she looked up—her eyes a clear, weary gray. "Thank you," she said, voice barely above a whisper. They spoke in fits and starts, conversation stuttering over the rain and the awkwardness of strangers. Her name was Maria. She had once worked as an assistant in a law office, but after a sudden round of layoffs, she lost her apartment, unable to navigate the maze of social support. "It happened so fast," she murmured. "One missed paycheck, then everything slipped away."

Kevin listened as she described nights spent searching for safe places to sleep, the humiliation of invisible poverty, the indifference of passersby. He felt the chill seep into his bones—not from the rain, but from the realization that her story was not an anomaly but a recurring thread in the tapestry of the city. As he walked home, her words echoed in his mind, refusing to be drowned out by the city's incessant noise.

The Scales Fall

Back in his apartment, Kevin stared at the spreadsheets scattered across his table. Where he once saw only numbers, he now glimpsed lives—hopes deferred, opportunities denied, the consequences of choices made in boardrooms far from the street. The figures were not abstract; they were a ledger of injustice, each data point a testament to a system's failure. The discomfort that had shadowed him became indignation, a burning need to act.

He realized, with a mix of horror and revelation, that the financial instruments he had mastered could be turned to another purpose. Hidden within the labyrinth of derivatives and equities was a flaw—a vulnerability that, if exploited, could disrupt the machinery of the elite. The thought was electric, both terrifying and exhilarating. For the first time, he saw a path toward rebalancing the scales, toward giving voice to those silenced by circumstance.

Formulating a Plan: The War Room

Sleep eluded Kevin as he poured over economic data, his apartment transformed into a command center. Post-its littered his walls, crisscrossed with lines and annotations; books on market theory and regulatory law bristled with bookmarks. He watched the markets as if seeking omens, searching for patterns that could be manipulated in favor of the many rather than the few.

He devised scenarios, tested hypotheses, simulated outcomes. The television played business news on a loop, analysts debating the next market bubble, the next political shakeup. Kevin ignored the noise, focusing instead on the underlying structures—the seams and fault lines that could be pried apart. He adopted the methods of those he sought to oppose: meticulous

research, patience, and the willingness to act boldly
when opportunity arose.

Tactics of the Elite

The more Kevin learned, the clearer the adversary
became. The wealthiest 1% did not simply benefit from
fortune; they sculpted it, using their resources to
influence policy, twist regulations, and control the flow
of information. Insider trading went unpunished, cloaked
in plausible deniability. Market manipulation became a
skill set, not a crime, with loopholes engineered into the
very framework of finance. Offshore accounts shielded
profits from taxation, while lobbying groups shaped
laws to maintain the status quo.

Kevin catalogued these tactics, building a dossier on the
architecture of global inequality. He saw how asset
bubbles were inflated, who benefited when they burst,
and how entire economies were held hostage to the

whims of a privileged few. The realization was infuriating—and galvanizing. If the rules of the game had been written to favor the elite, then perhaps the game itself could be subverted.

Reaching into the Underground

Kevin knew he could not wage this war alone. The scale of the challenge demanded allies: people with technical skill, street-level knowledge, and a willingness to risk everything for the promise of change. He turned to the digital underworld—anonymous forums where disillusioned professionals congregated, social media groups where activists exchanged coded messages, encrypted channels that buzzed with rumors of rebellion.

Carefully, he crafted his pitch, avoiding overt language that might attract the wrong kind of attention. He spoke of collective action, of using financial tools as weapons for justice, of leveling the playing field. Responses trickled in—some hostile, many skeptical, but a few curious, hungry for something to believe in. He arranged clandestine meetings in half-empty coffee shops, his identity shielded by layers of anonymity.

One by one, he assembled a motley crew: a data scientist from Mumbai, bitter at the offshoring of her job; a former trader from New York, wracked with guilt over the 2008 crash; a schoolteacher from Brixton, who moonlighted as a hacker. Each brought a different perspective, a different skill set, and each carried the scars of a world that had failed them. Trust was slow to build, eroded by past betrayals and the ever-present threat of surveillance.

## The Struggle for Unity

Recruitment was harder than he expected. Many potential allies recoiled at the idea of confronting the system head-on, scarred by years of disappointment and fear. Some accused Kevin of being a plant, a spy for the very powers he sought to undermine. Others simply could not believe that change was possible, their hope worn thin by years of neglect.

Still, Kevin persisted, forging connections through shared stories and late-night conversations. He listened as his comrades recounted their experiences—evictions, lost pensions, shattered dreams. Gradually, the group coalesced, bound not by ideology but by a common grievance and a flicker of ambition. They began to develop code words, secure protocols, a makeshift chain of command. What started as a loose network became something more: a nascent movement, a community of the desperate and the determined.

The Money War Begins

As dawn broke over London, the city washed clean by the night's storm, Kevin stood again at his window. He saw the world anew: a battlefield divided not by nation or creed but by access, by power, by the invisible hand that shaped destinies. Behind him, his apartment was littered with the detritus of planning, the air charged with anticipation. Before him lay uncertainty—and the possibility of revolution.

He was no longer alone. Together, he and his newfound allies would challenge the machinery of wealth, not with violence but with strategy, cunning, and unwavering resolve. The seed of discontent had taken root, nurtured by hardship and indignation. The money war was coming, and for the first time in a long while, hope felt real.

Part 2: Escalation

## The Battle Expands

The warehouse was thick with exhaustion—a haze that clung to every surface, every discarded coffee cup, every cluster of scrawled notes tacked to the makeshift war board. Kevin's team had spent weeks pressed beneath the weight of Blackwood's assault, every hour a contest of will and ingenuity against a relentless adversary. The victory they'd clawed from the jaws of defeat was real, yet it came at a cost. Faces once flush with adrenaline now sagged with fatigue; eyes that had burned with defiance now flickered with unease. The air trembled with the memory of close calls, sleepless nights, and the ceaseless pounding of financial warfare. They had survived—but only just.

Kevin stood at the center of the room, surveying his team with a strategist's gaze. Worry creased his brow.

The fight had battered them, but it had also revealed something vital—the battlefield was far larger than they'd imagined. Blackwood didn't play by borders, and neither could they. If their rebellion was to become more than a fleeting footnote in the annals of financial insurrection, it needed to break free from the confines of a single nation. The next move was clear: global expansion.

## Aftermath: The Toll of Victory

The days following their counterattack bled together in a blur of muted triumph and lingering dread. The team had succeeded, but the victory felt hollow—a pyrrhic conquest that left them sapped and wary. Each member bore the scars of the battle in their own way. Maria's usually steady hands now trembled over her keyboard; David, the architect of their most daring trades, was haunted by the constant need to anticipate, adapt, survive. Even the warehouse, once a sanctuary, now felt claustrophobic, the walls closing in as they waited for Blackwood's next move.

But as the adrenaline faded, resolve began to take its place. Kevin gathered the team for a midnight meeting, their faces illuminated by the glow of monitors and the city's distant lights. There, he shared his vision—a rebellion that would not cower behind borders, but would rise to meet the global forces aligned against them. "We can't win this war by playing small," he said, his voice steady despite the fatigue. "If we stay isolated, Blackwood will crush us. But if we build a network—if we spread our message and our methods—we can turn this fight into a movement."

Maria's Mission: Reaching Across Borders

No one was better suited to the task of global outreach than Maria. Her talent for anonymity, her labyrinthine contacts, and her fluency in the hidden languages of the web were their passport to the world. Working in the deep hours before dawn, Maria began to chart a new course. She reached out across continents—encrypted messages sent to sympathetic hackers in Berlin, whispered invitations left in the shadowy forums of Hong Kong, discreet requests for aid delivered to academics disillusioned by the status quo.

Her network responded. Messages trickled in from every corner of the globe, cautious at first, then bolder. Some were cryptic affirmations—an economist in South America pledging resources, a data scientist in Scandinavia offering analytic support. Others were more direct: "I have seen what Blackwood is capable of. I'm in."

New Allies: The Faces of the International Rebellion

With Maria's guidance, Kevin's team began to grow—not just in numbers, but in expertise and diversity. Each new member brought a unique strength and perspective, weaving the fabric of a truly global coalition.

Dr. Deitra Huhni: The Voice of Emerging Markets

Dr. Deitra Huhni arrived via encrypted video call, her presence calm and incisive. A renowned economist from the University of Delhi, Deitra had witnessed firsthand the havoc wrought by financial manipulation in developing economies. She spoke with quiet authority, outlining the vulnerabilities Blackwood exploited, the market signals he relied upon, and the ways local knowledge could turn these traps against him.

"Emerging markets aren't just pawns in this conflict," Deitra explained. "They can be weapons—if we know how to use them." She mapped out a series of trades and alliances, her strategies driven by a deep understanding of both numbers and people. Her arrival was a turning point. Kevin felt the weight lift, just a little, as the team gained not only an ally but a guide through unfamiliar terrain.

Professor John P. Dubois: Master of Global Trade

Next came Professor John P. Dubois, a dignified figure from the halls of the Sorbonne. Dubois had spent a lifetime dissecting the arteries of global commerce, tracing the flow of goods and capital with the precision of a surgeon. His insight was invaluable—he could spot the ripple effects of a trade war weeks before they broke the surface; he understood how a single shipment diverted could alter the balance of power.

Dubois brought more than expertise—he brought legitimacy. His connections among journalists, NGOs, and progressive politicians opened doors the team had never dreamed of. In his presence, the movement seemed to gain not just numbers, but gravitas. Even Blackwood, Kevin suspected, would take notice.

Hidondi Makama: The Guardian of Code

Last to join the inner circle was Hidondi Makama, a reclusive programmer from Tokyo whose mastery of cybersecurity bordered on the legendary. Makama spoke little, his words often lost behind layers of technical jargon, but his impact was felt immediately. He fortified their systems, deploying decentralized networks and encrypted channels, transforming their digital presence from a vulnerable network into a fortress. Blackwood's hackers found themselves rebuffed, their attacks losing steam against Makama's defenses.

Yet Hidondi was more than a shield—he was a weapon. He devised algorithms to track disinformation, bots to amplify the group's counter-narratives, and clandestine networks that allowed for peer-to-peer transactions beyond the reach of corrupt institutions. With Hidondi, the team could not only survive digital warfare—they could strike back.

## Building the Global Network

The team's expansion required more than new members; it demanded new infrastructure. The traditional banking system, with its roots sunk deep in the soil of the establishment, was vulnerable to manipulation. Blackwood's allies could freeze assets, intercept transactions, and monitor communications. Kevin's team needed a system that could not be contained.

Under Hidondi's guidance, they built an encrypted platform—secure, decentralized, and borderless. Peer-to-peer transactions flourished, enabling the rapid exchange of resources. Information, funds, and strategies flowed unimpeded, linking supporters from

Lagos to London, Buenos Aires to Beijing. This wasn't just a financial network—it was a movement, pulsing with the collective will of those determined to topple the old order.

## Blackwood's Counter-Offensive

Blackwood was not a man to accept defeat. His first wave of retaliation was subtle—a smear campaign launched through state-sponsored media, painting Kevin's movement as anarchists and destabilizers. Headlines screamed about shadowy cabals undermining global security. Political figures, lobbied by Blackwood's agents, called for crackdowns and new regulations.

But Blackwood's attacks did not stop with words. He wielded his influence to freeze accounts, block transfers, and have international financial watchdogs scrutinize every transaction linked to the network. He branded

Kevin's group as economic terrorists, hoping to force sympathetic governments to turn hostile.

The Team Responds: Data, Truth, and the War for Perception

Kevin and his allies refused to let Blackwood control the narrative. They launched a counter-campaign, using data analytics and rigorous economic research to dismantle his accusations. Led by Deitra and Dubois, the team published detailed reports—transparent, meticulously sourced, and immune to easy dismissal. Hidondi ensured their distribution via secure channels, while Maria orchestrated their amplification by sympathetic journalists and activists.

The reports did more than defend the movement—they turned the spotlight on Blackwood himself. Hidden transactions, conflicts of interest, and patterns of market manipulation were laid bare for the world to see. The hypocrisy of Blackwood's crusade became impossible to ignore. Public opinion, once easily swayed by fear, began to shift.

Financial Chess: Leveraging Global Expertise

The war evolved into a series of high-stakes maneuvers, each move calculated with surgical precision. With Deitra's help, the team exploited currency fluctuations in emerging markets, predicting shifts that Blackwood's agents couldn't see coming. Their trades yielded not just profit, but strategic advantage—funding new operations, expanding the network, and keeping their adversaries off balance.

Dubois's mastery of trade routes and international markets allowed Kevin's team to anticipate and counter Blackwood's gambits. When Blackwood tried to corner a vital resource, Dubois identified alternative suppliers and rerouted shipments, neutralizing the threat before it could materialize. Hidondi's monitoring systems flagged suspicious activity, giving David the information he needed to execute preemptive trades that turned Blackwood's own schemes against him.

Every victory was hard-won, every defeat a lesson. The team's adaptability became their greatest weapon. They learned to think like their enemy—anticipating, outmaneuvering, and seizing opportunities in the chaos Blackwood created.

## Challenges of Expansion

With every new member, the network's complexity grew. Cultural differences sometimes sparked misunderstandings—an offhand remark from Dubois that offended a South American partner, an encrypted message from Hidondi misinterpreted by a Nigerian analyst. The diversity that was their strength also required patience, diplomacy, and a willingness to learn.

Navigating the legal frameworks of dozens of countries was a constant challenge. Maria spent sleepless nights coordinating with attorneys and activists, ensuring that each transaction, each piece of communication, stayed just on the right side of the law. One misstep could expose the entire movement, hand Blackwood a weapon they could not afford to lose.

And yet, through it all, trust remained the glue that held the rebellion together. Every new ally was scrutinized, their motives weighed, their loyalties tested. Paranoia was a constant companion—one infiltrator could destroy everything. But slowly, bonds formed. The team became more than collaborators; they became comrades, united by a vision that transcended borders, languages, and backgrounds.

## The Movement Grows

As word spread of their successes, the movement swelled. What began as a handful of insurgents became a network of hundreds—then thousands. Grassroots organizations, reform-minded economists, even some disgruntled members of the financial elite found themselves drawn to Kevin's cause. The narrative shifted. Media outlets that once parroted Blackwood's accusations began to question the status quo, exploring the possibility of genuine reform.

Kevin found himself at the center of something larger than he'd ever imagined. He was no longer merely a strategist fighting to survive—he was the architect of a nascent revolution. The team's victories became rallying cries for justice. Their setbacks, lessons in resilience.

Climax: The Birth of a Revolution

The culminating moment arrived not with a single dramatic confrontation, but with a cascade of small triumphs that, together, signaled a seismic shift. Major news outlets ran stories questioning Blackwood's practices, using data provided by the team. Governments that had once condemned Kevin's movement began to quietly reach out, seeking counsel. The financial elite, sensing the winds of change, scrambled to adapt.

## Part 3: The Counteroffensive

### Shadows, Strategies, and the Spark of Revolution

### Aftermath of Defeat

The Swiss chalet—once alive with the ceaseless hum of ideas and the laughter of comrades—now lay suffused in a spectral quiet. Outside, the Alps stretched immaculate and indifferent, their peaks dusted with fresh snow that glowed blue in the dawn light. Within, only the soft hum of servers broke the silence. Every surface seemed to echo with the ghosts of triumphs now hollowed by loss.

Kevin sat at a window, his silhouette framed by frost-edged panes. His face was gaunt, eyes sunken from sleepless nights, his hands pressed to the glass as if searching the horizon for solace or a sign. The weight of recent defeats pressed upon him: not only the staggering financial blows but the more personal wounds—the betrayals of allies he once considered family. Trust had been ripped apart, leaving behind only suspicion and grief.

Deitra was a study in exhaustion and perseverance. Her fingers danced across her keyboard, eyes flickering with undimmed fire. There was a brittle edge to her voice when she spoke, as though every word was a test of will. Marcus, usually the room's spark, had become a figure hunched over a battered laptop, his energy now a quiet, feverish intensity. Silas, the silent sentinel, drifted in and out of rooms, always in the periphery—an embodiment of the sacrifices they had all made.

The air was thick with unspoken regrets and raw anxiety. Meals were taken in silence. Paranoia—the fear that another betrayal lay around every corner—was their constant companion. Yet beneath the pain, a fragile thread of resolve began to weave them together again.

Scars, Kevin realized, could be reminders not only of pain, but of survival.

## Strategic Rebirth

The first step out of despair was the hardest. It began with a simple statement, hoarse and uneven, that cut through the pall: "We need a new plan," Kevin said, voice weighted with fatigue and something sharper—determination. The others looked up, the flicker of hope barely perceptible but present.

The next days became an unrelenting crucible. They spent hours dissecting each past decision: reviewing encrypted message threads, financial transaction logs, and every point where Dense had anticipated or countered them. The walls of the chalet soon filled with whiteboards layered in diagrams, timelines, and color-coded risk assessments. Every late-night session was punctuated by heated debate—sometimes erupting into argument, sometimes descending into silence.

Deitra pushed for bolder, more visible action. "We were too subtle. He knows how to play in the shadows." She advocated for a campaign that would force Dense into the open, exposing him to scrutiny and vulnerability.

Marcus, ever the tactician, countered with a plea for precision. "If we go loud, we have to be surgical. We can't afford another misstep." He believed that their next move must be unpredictable—striking at Dense's soft spots with overwhelming force before he could adapt.

But it was Silas who reminded them of the stakes. "Every channel we use, every new recruit, is a possible entry point for a traitor." His warnings led to the implementation of rigorous security protocols and exhaustive background checks for anyone considered for the inner circle.

Their post-mortem revealed a critical vulnerability: concentration of assets and loyalty. Dense had exploited their reliance on a few key investments and trusted insiders, systematically dismantling their infrastructure. The new plan would be built on diversification and resilience, rooted in decentralization rather than hierarchy.

They mapped out four primary fronts:

- Direct Financial Assault: Targeting Dense's key holdings with high-risk, high-reward strategies—short-selling, leveraged options—designed to destabilize his empire. This would require substantial, carefully managed capital, pooled from a new network of allies.

- Public Exposure: Orchestrating the release of damning evidence across multiple media platforms. Every leak, every article, would be meticulously vetted for accuracy and impact, aiming to erode Dense's grip on public perception.

- Legal Pressure: Compiling and channeling evidence to trigger investigations across diverse regulatory environments. This would necessitate alliances with attorneys, watchdogs, and activists, each vetted for integrity and commitment to the cause.

- Internal Disruption: Identifying and cultivating contacts—disillusioned employees, ambitious executives—within Dense's organization, leveraging incentives and blackmail to sew seeds of discord and sabotage from within.

Morning blurred into night as they rehearsed scenarios, ran simulations, and argued over every contingency. The process was grueling. Trust, so easily shattered, was painstakingly rebuilt through candor and mutual sacrifice. It was in these fire-forged moments that the team rediscovered their purpose—not just as strategists or hackers, but as revolutionaries bound by a vision of justice.

## Technological Arms Race

The digital world became their new war zone—a theater of operations where Dense's old-world influence was less absolute. Marcus, drawing on his prowess as a coding prodigy, developed a suite of AI-driven tools. Chief among them was a sophisticated algorithmic network—part bot army, part social intelligence engine—designed to infiltrate, monitor, and manipulate social discourse with unprecedented subtlety.

These bots weren't the blunt instruments of populist campaigns; they were digital chameleons, capable of engaging in nuanced debates, amplifying dissent, and injecting subversive truths into the bloodstream of online communities. The code was so refined that even seasoned analysts struggled to distinguish fabricated dialogue from genuine grassroots sentiment.

Simultaneously, Deitra spearheaded the development of "Oracle," their flagship AI system. Oracle ingested terabytes of financial data—trading volumes, asset movements, market sentiment, and Dense's personal behavioral patterns—feeding it through neural networks trained to predict market shifts and Dense's own tactical decisions. Every output was scrutinized, every anomaly debated, until the system's forecasts became eerily accurate.

Oracle's greatest value lay not only in anticipating Dense's investments but in orchestrating counter-moves. If Oracle predicted a surge in a given commodity, they would engineer subtle market distortions—covertly buying and selling through shell accounts, tipping the scales just enough to throw Dense's strategies into chaos.

Silas's focus was fortifying their digital perimeter. Using a rotating network of encrypted servers, he deployed cutting-edge anonymization tools and built a labyrinth of virtual decoys—honeypots and sacrificial databases—that lured Dense's hackers into endless loops. Any successful breach yielded only meticulously crafted misinformation. True operations remained veiled behind layers of quantum-resistant encryption.

Cryptocurrency became both shield and sword. Silas designed decentralized funding protocols on custom blockchain platforms, allowing assets to flow seamlessly between trusted nodes. These transactions, masked by zero-knowledge proofs and multi-jurisdiction routing, rendered Dense's asset freezes and financial surveillance futile.

Every technological innovation was stress-tested under simulated attacks. Red team–blue team exercises became daily ritual, with Marcus launching creative assaults and Silas patching vulnerabilities in real time. Paranoia was not only tolerated—it was institutionalized, their best defense against an unseen adversary.

## Rebuilding the Movement

Power, they learned, could not survive in isolation. The team's next challenge was to reconstitute their movement—not as the centralized hierarchy Dense had exploited, but as a resilient, decentralized collective.

Recruitment became a discipline of its own. Prospective members were sourced from activist communities, underground financial networks, and whistleblower forums. Each underwent a rigorous, multi-layered vetting process: psychological screening, background checks, even polygraphs. Paranoia and pragmatism fused, forging a core group with unwavering loyalty.

Training was immersive and relentless. New members learned the intricacies of digital security, economic theory, and psychological operations. Weekly exercises simulated hostile infiltrations and counterintelligence maneuvers, building not only skills but a shared sense of mission.

Relationships with grassroots organizations were cultivated with care. Kevin, ever the diplomat, forged alliances with community leaders, reform-minded economists, and independent journalists. Each relationship was built on transparency, mutual respect, and a shared commitment to economic justice.

Decision-making shifted towards radical transparency. Every major initiative was debated and voted upon by the core group, and dissent was encouraged as a safeguard against groupthink. This open model, though sometimes slower, yielded more robust and resilient strategies.

The network's diversity, once a liability, became its greatest strength. Local teams adapted global strategies to suit regional nuances, creating a lattice of semi-autonomous cells united in purpose but free to innovate in execution.

## Public Awareness and Media Campaign

Their digital and financial campaigns, while potent, were incomplete without public support. Dense's empire thrived on opacity and narrative control. Winning required not just exposing truth but inspiring belief.

Deitra's analytical acumen identified segments of the population most affected by Dense's economic manipulations: the disenfranchised, the middle class squeezed by debt, and even certain segments of the financial elite wary of Dense's consolidation of power. Each group was targeted with custom-crafted messaging, the result of data-driven sentiment analysis and an intimate understanding of their fears and aspirations.

Marcus's innovations in social media engineering came to the fore. He designed viral content—memes, short documentaries, interactive infographics—that highlighted the human cost of corruption. These weren't mere propaganda: they were stories, painstakingly gathered from those devastated by economic disparity, designed to build empathy and outrage.

Campaigns were orchestrated for maximum impact: coordinated hashtags, synchronized video releases, and live Q&As with credible experts. Rather than descending into sensationalism, the team emphasized facts, transparency, and a vision for reform.

Dense fought back hard. His PR machines unleashed smear campaigns, saturating the media with doctored footage and manufactured scandals. But the team was ready. AI-powered fact-checking bots monitored news cycles in real time, flagging and debunking falsehoods before they could metastasize. Trusted third-party fact-checkers and independent journalists were brought in to verify and amplify corrections.

The public rallies that followed were unlike any in the movement's history. They were not only protests, but forums for financial literacy, empowerment, and collective action. Workshops taught participants how to spot financial fraud, protect assets, and organize local resistance. The events became fertile ground for new recruitment—and for the first time in months, hope became contagious.

## Global Expansion

Dense's influence spanned continents—a tangled web of shell companies, offshore accounts, and political backchannels. The team knew their campaign's success hinged on international escalation.

Kevin, with his knack for diplomacy, discreetly reached out to sympathetic officials in the International Monetary Fund, World Bank, and the European Central Bank. Rather than overwhelming these institutions with reams of evidence, he fed them carefully curated anomalies: unexplained transactions, irregular asset flows, and inconsistencies in Dense's reported holdings. Each breadcrumb was designed to trigger internal audits, not accusations.

Deitra's team aggregated financial intelligence from sources in multiple time zones, cross-referencing data leaks with real-time market data. Patterns emerged—proof of global-scale money laundering and collusion. This information was selectively leaked to investigative journalists renowned for independence and rigor. Off-the-record briefings provided frameworks for investigation without tipping Dense to the team's involvement.

As stories began to break in The Financial Times, Le Monde, and The New York Times, whispers of corruption transformed into calls for inquiry. The Swiss

Federal Banking Commission became the first domino to fall, launching an investigation after uncovering a minor discrepancy in an offshore transaction. The inquiry expanded, revealing a complex web of shell companies and unreported assets. Soon after, parallel investigations sprouted in the UK, US, and several EU nations.

Diplomatic pressure mounted. Governments once cowed by Dense's reach began to distance themselves, issuing cautious statements and requesting clarity on the allegations. Emergency summits were convened. The G20 agenda shifted to include anti-corruption reforms—a public signal that the tide was turning.

## Escalating Conflict

Dense was not a passive adversary. His countermeasures were swift and ruthless. He unleashed waves of cyberattacks—phishing campaigns, DDoS blitzes, and sophisticated malware—intended to cripple the team's infrastructure and expose their leadership. Silas's defensive architecture held, with only minor breaches yielding pre-planted misinformation.

The psychological war intensified. Dense's operatives sought to infiltrate the movement with double agents and spread paranoia through anonymous threats and disinformation. Every new member was scrutinized; encrypted channels buzzed with warnings and verification protocols. The emotional toll was immense—trust, always fragile, was stretched to breaking.

Marcus, tasked with counter-espionage, turned their own toolkit inward—monitoring message traffic for anomalies, tracking suspicious access patterns, and running regular "integrity audits" on both code and personnel. False positives occasionally triggered panic, but these drills became opportunities to reinforce discipline and unity.

But Dense's greatest weapon remained public narrative. His media allies painted Kevin's movement as reckless radicals, intent on destabilizing world markets. Old scandals were dredged up, images doctored, family members threatened. Deitra endured anonymous death threats; Silas's relatives were harassed online. Kevin took these attacks personally, fearing for the safety of everyone who had committed to the cause.

Still, the team adapted. Marcus's social bots flooded forums with evidence-based rebuttals and real testimonials. Silas organized a campaign to expose the mechanics of Dense's propaganda, deconstructing smear tactics in real time. They turned defense into offense— transforming attacks into teachable moments for their growing audience.

Internationally, alliances began to fracture. Dense's former partners, fearing implication, leaked their own evidence to authorities in exchange for immunity. The net was tightening.

## The Geneva Showdown

The crescendo of their long campaign arrived in a conference room overlooking Lake Geneva. The room was suffused with late afternoon light, the air electric with expectation and dread. Kevin, Deitra, and Marcus took their places opposite Dense and his team—a phalanx of high-priced attorneys and lobbyists.

Dense looked diminished, his once-imposing frame shrouded in arrogance now tattered by fear. His gaze was icy, but his composure brittle—cracks visible to anyone who cared to look. Kevin, calm but hard as steel, met his eyes with unflinching resolve. Months of preparation had led to this moment.

The proceedings began with Dense's lawyers attempting to discredit the evidence: questioning the authenticity of documents, impugning the motives of witnesses, and casting aspersions on the investigative process. But Kevin's team had anticipated every move. Deitra presented market data in real time—projecting live graphs that illustrated the ripple effects of Dense's manipulations, connecting dots that no amount of obfuscation could erase.

Marcus maintained a secure channel with international regulators and journalists, relaying updates and ensuring the meeting's integrity. Every time Dense's team attempted to disrupt or delay, they were met with calmly presented, irrefutable facts—each piece of evidence independently verified by multiple agencies and corroborated by whistleblower testimony.

The turning point came when Deitra's team, working with Swiss authorities, unveiled records of a previously undiscovered offshore account in the Cayman Islands. The account contained billions, the proceeds of decades of fraud, tax evasion, and market manipulation. The discovery stunned even Dense's defenders. With nowhere left to hide, Dense's facade finally crumbled.

International representatives, at first cautious, now voiced outrage and condemnation. The cumulative weight of evidence and diplomatic pressure was insurmountable. Dense's last gambit—a teary plea of innocence, a calculated attempt to shift blame—was met with silence. The decision was unanimous: legal proceedings would commence against Dense and his associates, their assets frozen, their influence shattered.

## Resolution

There was no moment of raucous celebration—only a quiet, exhausted release. The team stood together, watching as the sun set behind the mountains, their faces illuminated by the glow of a future they had fought to reclaim. Their victory was not just over a single corrupt man, but over the structures that enabled him—a triumph of transparency, collaboration, and the refusal to be cowed by power.

Word of Dense's defeat reverberated across the globe. Markets surged, then stabilized; regulatory reforms moved from aspiration to law. Grassroots movements, emboldened by the victory, sprang up in cities across continents. The team's innovations—open-source cybersecurity tools, encrypted communication networks, financial literacy programs—were adopted by activists and reformers, empowering a new generation to resist exploitation.

For Kevin, Deitra, Marcus, and Silas, the victory was bittersweet. The cost had been immense—relationships lost, innocence shattered, paranoia ingrained. Yet as they watched the movement swell beyond anything they could have imagined, they understood that their pain had not been in vain. They had lit a fire that would not easily be extinguished.

The road ahead would be fraught with new challenges: the remnants of Dense's empire, the slow machinations of justice, the risk of backlash from those who had profited from the old order. But for the first time, hope was not a fragile thing. It was a force, woven into the fabric of a new world.

As the team left Geneva, a single phrase echoed among them: the fight for economic justice was not over, but it was now truly possible. They had proved that even the most powerful could be brought to account, that ordinary people—when united, determined, and unafraid—could reshape the destiny of nations.

Part 4: Justice and Aftermath

The Trial of Henry Dense and the Dawn of a New Era

Prelude to Justice

The echoes of the Geneva meeting still reverberated in the minds of all who had witnessed its revelations. For Kevin Henden, Deitra Huhni, and Marcus Riley, the whirlwind that followed was not a moment of rest, but the threshold of a greater, more daunting challenge. Geneva had been the public unmasking, a meticulously orchestrated prelude—the overture to a drama whose true stage awaited in the austere courtrooms of international justice.

In those hours after Dense's façade crumbled, the world watched, spellbound. Market screens flashed with surges of hope and fear, news tickers rolled Dense's name across every continent, and grassroots activists flooded the streets, their voices rising in a chorus of vindication. But for the trio at the heart of the storm, there was no time for celebration. Within hours, they were swept into a maelstrom of legal depositions, urgent strategy sessions, and ceaseless communication with allies across the world. Every document, every scrap of evidence painstakingly gathered over months and years, now had to withstand the fierce scrutiny of international law.

The transition was both physical and psychological—a shift from the glare of Geneva's conference halls to the dim, imposing courtrooms of The Hague, London, Zurich, and New York. Here, the rules were different, the stakes higher, and the cost of error far greater. The coming battle would not be fought in the open, but under the unyielding gaze of judges, prosecutors, and adversaries determined to reclaim lost ground. The team's unity was absolute; their resolve sharpened by the knowledge that the outcome would shape the fate of more than just a criminal—this trial would chart the course of the world's future.

The Legal Battle

The proceedings began with Dense's formidable legal team launching a barrage of attacks. Their strategy was familiar: sow doubt, discredit witnesses, and challenge the very foundations of the evidence. In one hearing after another, they questioned the authenticity of documents, impugned the motives of whistleblowers, and cast aspersions on the investigative process. Their arguments were elegant, their rhetoric sharp—but against them stood a wall of preparation, forged in the crucible of adversity.

Kevin's team had anticipated every maneuver. Deitra, with a calm precision that belied the gravity of the moment, projected live graphs and financial models for the court, connecting the dots of Dense's manipulations in real time. The data, sourced from international markets and verified by multiple agencies, became a language that even the most skeptical found impossible to ignore. The cascading lines of loss and profit, the unexpected ripples in obscure markets—all traced to Dense's hidden hand—were laid bare for the world to see.

Marcus, ever vigilant, maintained a secure channel with regulators and journalists across continents. Each time Dense's team attempted to delay or disrupt, they were met with facts—presented calmly, unwaveringly, and always corroborated by a chorus of independent voices. The courtrooms, usually places of ambiguity and debate, became theaters of inevitability. Every fact, every testimony, was a blow against the edifice of Dense's carefully constructed lies.

The drama reached its zenith when, in cooperation with Swiss authorities, Deitra's team unveiled records of a previously undiscovered offshore account in the Cayman Islands. The account, a cipher behind layers of legal obfuscation, revealed billions in hidden assets—decades of fraud, tax evasion, and market manipulation made manifest in black and white. Even Dense's defenders were momentarily stunned. The realization that no stone had been left unturned shattered the last illusions of Dense's invulnerability.

## The Unraveling

As the trial unfolded, Dense's strategy of deflection and denial quickly unraveled. His legal team's attempts to conjure conspiracies, to paint their client as a victim of political vendetta, wilted under the relentless progression of evidence. One by one, the dominos fell: encrypted communications, decrypted by Marcus's security experts, exposed a labyrinthine network of bribery and collusion that reached into the highest echelons of government, business, and even international organizations. The evidence was not just damning—it was exhaustive.

Deitra's testimony, delivered with quiet authority, laid out the impact of Dense's crimes in devastating detail. Market manipulation, predatory lending, the systematic exploitation of vulnerable populations—each scheme mapped, modeled, and quantified. She spoke not as a prosecutor seeking vengeance, but as an analyst revealing the cost in shattered lives and hollowed communities. The faces of jurors, journalists, and even seasoned legal professionals betrayed shock as the scale of Dense's enterprise became clear.

Kevin, who had once thrived on abstract financial theories, now became a masterful translator for the world. He broke down complex data into accessible narratives, employing charts and vivid storytelling to render Dense's crimes in human terms. His words, delivered with a passion that cut through legal jargon, carried the jury and the public alike. The trial was no longer merely a reckoning for one man; it was a referendum on an entire system of unchecked greed.

Every day, the world's eyes turned to the courtroom. As Marcus quietly ensured the safety of his friends and the integrity of their operation, international media dissected each revelation. Scandals erupted as names once untouchable were linked to Dense's schemes. Reputations crumbled; careers ended overnight. Public trust in venerable institutions was shaken to its core. The courtroom became the crucible in which the future of the global economy would be forged.

## Sentencing and Consequences

The sentencing was a moment that transcended law and became legend. Dense, once the personification of untouchable power, now stood diminished—his posture stooped, his voice hollow. The judge's words were both indictment and epitaph, cataloging not just the crimes but their consequences: the stolen futures of millions, the distortion of markets, the corrosion of democracy. The sentence was unambiguous and severe—lengthy prison terms for Dense and his inner circle, crushing fines, and the seizure of assets on a scale not seen in modern history.

As the gavel fell, silence swept the courtroom. Outside, the world exhaled. In that single verdict, a message was sent that would echo for generations: no one, however powerful, is above the law. The system that had cowered before Dense now stood taller, its authority restored not by force, but by the relentless pursuit of truth.

## Ripple Effects

The immediate aftermath was electric. Governments convened emergency sessions. Regulatory bodies launched sweeping reviews. The international community, galvanized by the example set in Dense's trial, enacted a wave of reforms. Tax havens—those shadowy refuges for illicit wealth—were pierced by new transparency initiatives. Countries began sharing financial data, breaking the chains of secrecy that had long enabled the world's wealthiest to hide their assets.

Stringent regulations forced corporations and individuals to disclose holdings and transactions with unprecedented clarity. The era of invisible money, of hidden fortunes and untraceable transfers, was at an end. Governments saw a dramatic surge in tax revenue, resources that were swiftly channeled into education, healthcare, and public infrastructure. The very populations once exploited by Dense now began to reap the dividends of justice.

But the reforms did not stop at taxation. Predatory lending practices, responsible for years of hardship and exploitation, were brought to heel. New laws capped interest rates and demanded proof of creditworthiness, curbing the spread of debt traps. Microfinance initiatives, many seeded with the assets confiscated from Dense and his associates, blossomed around the world. For the first time, small businesses and entrepreneurs in developing regions found doors open to them, capital within reach.

A new architecture of oversight and accountability took root. Independent bodies, insulated from political and corporate influence, were empowered to monitor markets, investigate malfeasance, and mete out penalties. The days of reckless speculation and insider dealing faded, replaced with a culture of transparency and risk-aversion that stabilized markets and inspired investor confidence.

Of course, these changes did not come without resistance. The powerful, accustomed to unchecked prerogative, fought back with every tool at their disposal—lobbyists, legal challenges, and backroom deals. But the tide of public opinion, swelled by the drama of Dense's fall, proved unstoppable. Demonstrations, petitions, and viral media campaigns demanded accountability and reform. For the first time in decades, the will of the people pressed harder than the machinations of elites.

Global Transformation

What began as an isolated prosecution blossomed into a movement. International cooperation, once an elusive ideal, became a necessity. Agreements were forged to harmonize regulations, close loopholes, and prevent corporations from fleeing reform by shifting operations across borders. The formation of the Global Economic Reform Council (GERC)—a diverse coalition of economists, technologists, lawyers, and social activists—created the institutional muscle for lasting change.

The GERC's mandate was sweeping: to rebuild the very infrastructure of the global economy. Deitra, now internationally regarded for her mastery of sustainable finance, shaped policies that prioritized inclusive growth and environmental stewardship. Her vision gave rise to a network of community banks, built on microfinance principles, that offered credit, education, and financial empowerment to those long excluded from the system. These banks became engines of social development, resilient to shocks and deeply rooted in the communities they served.

Technology, once Dense's instrument of control, was repurposed as a tool of liberation. Deitra's team built secure, user-friendly platforms that democratized access to financial tools and resources. Blockchain technology, deployed at scale, ensured that every transaction was transparent, every asset accounted for. The shadowy world of backroom deals and whispered secrets was flooded with the light of public scrutiny.

Regulatory reforms extended to the heart of the corporate world. New laws targeted money laundering, tax evasion, and environmental malfeasance. Corporate accountability was no longer a slogan but a legal requirement, enforced by penalties severe enough to deter even the boldest would-be offenders. At every turn, the GERC's work was challenged by vested interests, but the support of an awakened and informed citizenry made backsliding politically perilous.

Education became the foundation on which the new order was built. Kevin, recognizing the power of knowledge, spearheaded the development of comprehensive financial literacy curricula. These programs, rolled out in schools and community centers worldwide, went beyond budgeting and investment—they instilled ethical awareness and critical thinking, preparing a new generation to make informed, responsible decisions. The goal was not just to empower individuals, but to inoculate society against the return of the old order.

The media, liberated from the grip of elite interests, flourished as an independent force for accountability. Investigative journalism thrived. Public debates on economic policy became fixtures of civic life. Through these channels, the spirit of reform was kept alive, and the failures and successes of the new system were scrutinized for all to see.

## Character Reflections

For Kevin, the journey was both a victory and a reckoning. The fight had cost him dearly—relationships strained, innocence lost, and a new wariness embedded in his soul. Yet, as he turned his energy from battle to construction, he found purpose in mentorship and policy. No longer the brash disruptor, he became the architect and guide, shaping systems to endure beyond the reach of any one individual.

Deitra, whose code and conviction had illuminated Dense's darkest secrets, now stood at the forefront of a revolution in finance. The community banks and platforms she designed were more than mechanisms— they were lifelines, pathways for millions toward economic security and dignity. Her work was grounded in the memory of past hardship, but her vision was always forward-looking: a world where prosperity was a right, not a privilege.

Marcus, having played the shadow strategist in the trials, now emerged as a builder of consensus and trust. His years of navigating political intrigue proved invaluable as he negotiated alliances, brokered compromises, and marshaled support for reforms among wary governments and institutions. The work was slower, less dramatic, but in its own way, more profound. He understood that victory in battle was just the beginning; real transformation required patience, persistence, and the courage to believe in possibility.

Together, their arcs reflected the transformation of the world itself: from confrontation to collaboration, from the pursuit of justice to the construction of a just society.

## Societal Shift

The ripple effects of Dense's downfall reshaped not only institutions, but the very fabric of society. Businesses, once measured solely by profit, were now compelled to consider their social and environmental impact. Consumers, emboldened by their new knowledge and civic engagement, demanded transparency from those who wished to earn their trust. Ethical investment became not just fashionable, but fundamental.

The education system, once focused on rote learning and narrow expertise, was overhauled to incorporate financial literacy and critical analysis. Schoolchildren learned not just how to balance a budget, but how markets functioned, how inequality emerged, and how their choices shaped the world around them. This new curriculum fostered a sense of global citizenship—and, more importantly, of responsibility.

In communities once scarred by exploitation, the impact was tangible. Grassroots initiatives flourished, supported by microloans and financial education. Local economies sprang to life, driven by entrepreneurship and mutual support. For many, it was the first taste of hope in generations.

The media, now a pillar of the new order, played its part with vigor—informing the public, exposing abuses, and ensuring that leaders, old and new, could not operate in darkness. The empowered citizenry, vigilant and informed, became the ultimate safeguard against the return of the old ways.

Enduring Legacy

The years following Dense's conviction were not without struggle. Old habits died hard, and powerful adversaries continued to search for weaknesses in the new system. There were setbacks—scandals, failed experiments, moments when the specter of the past seemed poised to return. But at each juncture, the unity of ordinary people, now equipped with knowledge and agency, carried the day.

Kevin, Deitra, and Marcus watched as their work blossomed beyond their expectations. They became mentors, symbols, and guardians of a dream that refused to die. Their story was told and retold—from classrooms to boardrooms, from city squares to remote villages. Each retelling was a reminder that power, unchecked, would always breed corruption—but that, united, people could reclaim their future.

The legacy of Geneva, of the trial that brought down a titan, endured in every reform, every new law, every citizen empowered to question and to act. Dense's name faded into history, a cautionary tale, while the movement he inadvertently inspired became the foundation for a world where justice, equity, and hope were more than words—they were lived realities.

And so, as the sun set behind distant mountains and rose again over cities reborn, the struggle continued. The fight for economic justice was far from over, but it was, at last, truly possible—a force woven into the fabric of a new world, driven not by fear, but by the unquenchable light of human hope.

Part 5: The Long Game

## The Challenge of Rebirth and the Relentless Pursuit of Justice

### Prelude to Reconstruction

The dust of revolution had barely settled when the world awoke to the magnitude of the challenge before it. The spectacle of Henry Dense brought to justice—a titan toppled, a corrupt apparatus exposed for all to see—was a watershed. But in the hush that followed celebration, reality set in. The old order's collapse had left a vacuum, and the war for a fairer world had only just begun.

Kevin Henden, physically and emotionally drained, stood at the crossroads of history. He had been the movement's spark—the orator, the strategist, the one who, with fiery conviction, called the powerless to action. Now, with the enemy vanquished, he found his role transformed. The time of upheaval was over; the time of construction had arrived. Kevin had become the architect, charged with laying the foundations of a society resilient against the ghosts of its past.

The Birth of the GERC

The first order of business was clear: build new institutions, not on the ashes of the old, but upon principles capable of withstanding the temptations of power. Thus was born the Global Economic Reform Council (GERC). It wasn't a haphazard amalgam of hopefuls; its membership was meticulously selected—economists, legal scholars, technologists, social activists—all united by a vision of justice, diversity, and transparency.

GERC's structure was revolutionary. Power was deliberately fragmented. Each committee, each decision, each transaction was scrutinized, documented, and made available to the public in real time. Deitra Huhni, whose expertise spanned sustainable finance and digital innovation, was instrumental. She designed systems for transparency and equity, intertwining environmental stewardship with economic growth, ensuring that the financial network was not only accountable but also resilient to abuse.

Marcus Riley, the group's seasoned diplomat, was the bridge-builder. He recognized that legitimacy required more than virtuous leadership; it demanded the trust and cooperation of governments, international bodies, and the very communities these reforms were meant to uplift. Marcus's years spent navigating political minefields became invaluable as he brokered alliances, negotiated with skeptics, and soothed the fears of those scarred by the old regime.

The Engines of Change: Community Empowerment and Education

The GERC's vision extended well beyond the reform of centralized institutions. Inspired by Deitra's microfinance models, they established community banks across continents—especially in regions left behind by globalization. These banks were more than conduits for credit; they became epicenters of local economic revival, offering financial literacy training and incubating new businesses. Entrepreneurship flourished. For the first time, marginalized communities gained the agency to shape their own destinies.

Education, Kevin believed, was the true lever of change. He spearheaded the development of curricula that reached from urban metropolises to rural outposts. The goal was not just to teach budgeting and investment but to foster critical thought, ethical reasoning, and an appreciation for how personal choices rippled through the wider world. Financial literacy was democratized, and so too, over time, was opportunity.

Technology as a Double-Edged Sword

Unlike Dense's regime, which used technology as a tool of control, GERC deployed it for empowerment. Deitra's team built open-access platforms that put powerful financial tools in the hands of ordinary people—no matter their resources or location. Peer-to-peer networks blossomed, and blockchain technology was harnessed for its transparency, not its obscurity. No more hidden transactions. No more untouchable elites. Every stakeholder could trace the flow of money, ensuring accountability at every link in the chain.

Yet, as the GERC soon discovered, innovation brought new dangers. The very algorithms designed to root out fraud could be exploited by those seeking to manipulate markets. Sophisticated actors—sometimes masquerading as philanthropists—used technology to mask new forms of exploitation. The GERC found itself waging a battle not only for financial justice but for control over the tools that made such justice possible.

Building a New Legal Order

GERC's mandate extended to the legal arena. Working hand-in-hand with the United Nations, the International Monetary Fund, and the World Bank, GERC developed a set of international regulations targeting the old system's most egregious abuses: tax havens, money laundering, regulatory arbitrage. The aim was to shut down the loopholes that had enabled the accumulation of unchecked wealth. Corporate social and environmental responsibility was enshrined in law.

These efforts were not without opposition. Powerful interests, both national and global, mounted fierce lobbying campaigns, seeking to water down reforms. But this time, with an empowered, informed public—bolstered by the GERC's relentless transparency and media literacy initiatives—the old guard found itself outmatched.

The Role of Media and Public Engagement

A rejuvenated media landscape became an essential pillar of the new order. Investigative journalists, emboldened by new protections and resources, exposed abuses wherever they surfaced. The GERC actively promoted critical engagement with news and information, training citizens to discern fact from propaganda. Informed civil society, rather than docile consumers, became the GERC's greatest ally and defense.

Still, the transition was anything but smooth. The beneficiaries of the old system resisted, sometimes violently. Sabotage, disinformation, and even physical threats became common. But the GERC's commitment to openness, inclusivity, and the tangible benefits of reform—greater access to credit, better education, narrowing inequality—gradually won over skeptics and built a durable social contract.

From Local Reform to Global Collaboration

The GERC's ambitions were always global, and Marcus Riley understood that success hinged on genuine international partnership. Utopian ideals were not enough; each victory required the slow, patient work of coalition-building. Scandinavian nations became early allies, lending legitimacy and practical expertise. Their experience managing robust welfare systems and fostering inclusive growth informed many of GERC's policies.

Conferences became crucibles of consensus, bringing together not just leaders but voices from civil society and the grassroots. The council entered into partnerships with international organizations and slowly won over skeptics—often by demonstrating how equitable reforms could foster stability and growth.

Deitra played a critical role in assuaging the concerns of developing nations, many of whom feared that reforms would simply entrench old inequalities in new forms. She designed capacity-building programs, technological assistance initiatives, and equitable resource distribution schemes that prioritized those long excluded from the global marketplace.

Technology again became the great enabler: secure, encrypted platforms allowed for genuine collaborative decision-making among widely dispersed members.

Blockchain technology, once feared as a tool for secrecy, now guaranteed transparency and accountability.

Legally, the GERC oversaw the drafting of new treaties and the creation of an international court to adjudicate disputes related to economic justice. The council's approach sought to level the playing field for all— eliminating legal havens and ensuring that the wealthy could no longer evade their responsibilities.

## Technological Revolution and Its Consequences

Deitra's team revolutionized global finance. Blockchain technology provided an auditable, tamper-proof ledger of transactions, undermining the old world's system of shell corporations and hidden assets. Artificial intelligence, trained on vast troves of historical data, became a shield against newly sophisticated forms of financial crime.

But technological democratization had unpredictable effects. Mobile banking applications—simple, multilingual, and adapted to local cultures—brought financial services to billions previously excluded. Yet, the rapid influx of new users strained infrastructure and created opportunities for predatory practices, forcing the GERC to develop stronger consumer protections without stifling innovation.

The interconnectedness of the new ecosystem, while enabling cross-border remittances and economic integration, also exposed the system to new risks. Cybersecurity became a top priority, with GERC investing in advanced encryption, AI-based defense systems, and international cooperation to combat cyberthreats. Public outreach campaigns explained both the benefits and limitations of the new technology, fostering trust and widespread adoption.

Privacy concerns became acute. While transparency was essential, individual rights also had to be protected. The GERC created independent oversight bodies and worked with privacy experts to ensure that data protection standards were rigorously enforced.

The need for constant innovation led to the creation of a dedicated R&D arm within the GERC, staffed by global experts and charged with anticipating threats and refining solutions as the digital landscape evolved.

## The Unintended Aftershocks

Success bred new challenges. Highly skilled cyber-attackers—sometimes state-sponsored, sometimes the last defenders of the old order—targeted GERC's financial systems. The arms race between defenders and adversaries intensified, shifting the battleground to the digital realm.

Financial inclusion, while largely positive, also opened the door for unscrupulous micro-lenders and new forms of financial exploitation. Overwhelmed infrastructure required massive investments in capacity and personnel. As wealth redistribution progressed, some nations—reliant on the inequities of the old system—responded with protectionism and covert sabotage.

Automation and AI, for all their promise, led to job displacement and social anxiety. The GERC responded with retraining programs and the creation of new industries. Nonetheless, the transition was turbulent, and the specter of unemployment threatened social stability.

Inequality lingered, transformed but not eradicated. The GERC's policies shifted towards wealth redistribution, progressive taxation, and the establishment of social safety nets. Fiscal fairness, too, required relentless adaptation, as new loopholes and evasions arose to replace those closed by reform.

Even with transparency, ethical dilemmas abounded. Where did the line lie between the public's right to know and individual privacy? The GERC walked a tightrope, adjusting regulations and procedures in response to emerging challenges.

Most critically, the success of reform depended not just on technical innovation but on the cultivation of a global ethic—a sense of shared responsibility for the future.

The Reality of the Long Game

Kevin's office, spare and contemplative, became both command center and sanctuary. He watched the world's transformation with a mixture of pride and anxiety. The city-scape beyond his window was a mosaic of hope and hardship—a vivid reminder that reform was a process, not an event.

The challenges he now faced were not the overt, brute force tactics of Dense's era but sophisticated, subtle campaigns leveraging technology, market manipulation, and social engineering. Shadowy actors exploited the very tools GERC had pioneered, seeking not just profit but the return of an inequitable order.

Kevin found himself at the nexus of economics, technology, and geopolitics. The global landscape, once unified in the pursuit of justice, now fractured under the strain of competing interests and renewed nationalism. He spent countless hours in delicate negotiations, balancing idealism with realpolitik, forming alliances with those willing to embrace change and countering the sabotage of those who resisted.

Data, once the harbinger of democratization, threatened to become overwhelming. Regulating the torrent of information, detecting manipulation, and maintaining public trust became daily battles. As the world's financial literacy improved, so too did the sophistication of those seeking to game the system.

Beyond policy and regulation lay the human element. The displacement of workers by automation required not just new jobs but a cultural shift towards adaptability and lifelong learning. The ethical dilemmas of AI—potential bias, privacy risks—demanded robust oversight and the constant refinement of trust frameworks.

Kevin understood, perhaps more than anyone, that the 'long game' was not a single campaign but a marathon without end. Each success revealed new vulnerabilities; each challenge demanded both humility and resolve. Yet, despite setbacks and disappointments, his belief in the vision—a world where wealth was not a zero-sum game, where opportunity was truly universal—remained unshaken.

He drew strength from his allies—Deitra and Marcus, each in their own realm, continuing to innovate, negotiate, and educate. The movement had outgrown its founders, becoming a global force for progress. Its stories were told in classrooms and town halls, reminders that the fight for justice was never truly won, only advanced.

As night fell and city lights flickered to life, Kevin steeled himself for the next day's battles. The era of easy victories was over; this was the hard, slow work of civilization. Yet in the quiet persistence of hope, he saw the promise that had animated the movement from the start.

The Unfinished Symphony

The struggle for economic justice had entered a more complex phase. No longer a story of heroes and villains, it had become a test of endurance, adaptability, and vision. The GERC's revolution was not just in its policies but in its process—a ceaseless commitment to transparency, inclusion, and the upliftment of all.

The long game stretched ahead, its outcome uncertain but its necessity undeniable. For Kevin, Deitra, Marcus, and millions more, the lesson was clear: the work of justice is never finished. It is a legacy not of perfection, but of persistence, a testament to the enduring power of human hope.

www.ingramcontent.com/pod-product-compliance
Lightning Source LLC
Chambersburg PA
CBHW071133100726
47908CB00008B/2586